Hay field

Barn yard

Corn crib

Wagon shed

Corn field

Milk Stand

Pasture

Garden

Milk house

Back Road — To Pasture and Wood Lot

Farmer Small's Farm
as seen by the eye of a Bird

The Little Farm

# THE
# LITTLE FARM

# LOIS LENSKI

Random House 🏠 New York

Farmer Small lives
on a farm.
He gets up early
in the morning.

He goes to the barn
to feed the animals.
They are all very
hungry.

He milks the cows.

He strains the milk
into the milk cans.
He sets them in the
milk cooler.

Farmer Small takes the cows to pasture.

Farmer Small leaves
the cans of milk
on the milk stand.
The milk truck takes them
to the dairy.

Farmer Small
    feeds the pigs.
They are
    very hungry!

So are
   the chickens,
   the ducks,
   and
      the turkeys!

At noon,
Farmer Small goes
    to the mailbox
    and gets his mail.

Farmer Small
has a tractor
to help him
with his work.

In the spring,
Farmer Small plows
the field
with his tractor.

He harrows
the field
with his tractor.

In the summer,
Farmer Small
cuts his hay
with his tractor.

He hauls the loads of hay
to the barn.

In the fall,
Farmer Small
   picks apples
   in his orchard.

He hauls them
    in the trailer
        behind the tractor.

He sells them
at his
roadside stand.

In the winter,
   Farmer Small
      chops his firewood.

He hauls the wood
on his bobsled
with his team.

Each day,
when evening comes,
Farmer Small gathers
the eggs.

He brings the cows
in from the pasture
and milks them.

Then
he goes into the house
to eat his supper—
and the sun goes down.

*And that's all—
about
Farmer Small!*

Hay field

Barn yard

Wagon shed

Corn crib

Corn field

Milk Stand

Pasture

Garden

Milk house

Back Road ~ To Pasture and Wood Lot

Farmer Small's Farm
as seen by the eye of a Bird